Lifeless

Lifeless

by Brandon Bowman

Principal PRINCIPLES

UNITED STATES OF AMERICA

Brandon Bowman, Author
bbowman.author@gmail.com

https://sites.google.com/view/brandon-bowman-books/

Publisher's Note: This is a work of fiction. Names, characters,
places, and incidents are a product of the author's imagination.
Locales and public names are sometimes used for atmospheric
purposes. Any resemblance to actual people, living or dead, or to
businesses, companies, events, institutions, or locales is completely coincidental.

Book design © 2017, BookDesignTemplates.com

Ordering Information: Special discounts are available on quantity
purchases by corporations, associations, and others. For details,
contact the publisher at the address above.

Brandon Bowman — First Edition

Print ISBN 978-1-7346374-3-4

eBook ISBN 978-1-7346374-5-8

Printed in the United States of America

Dedication

This book is dedicated to Dr. Lashaway-Bokina. I will never forget the way you encouraged and inspired me to become an author. You went above and beyond for me, and I wouldn't be here without you. I will always appreciate you.

Contents

CHAPTER 1

Just Doesn't Make Sense

Bruised. Beaten. Lifeless. The words kept ringing in my ears as if a loud cannon had just gone off. I couldn't imagine how not just one, but two men could leave another man nearly dead on the side of a road. This couldn't have actually happened, right?

"But how could they?" I asked. "How could they walk right by him?"

"That's a great question, Brandon," Mrs. Porter replied. "Maybe they were late for something. Maybe they thought they had something more important to do. Or maybe they just thought, surely someone else would take care of it. After all, they didn't even know the man."

Unlike every other Sunday school story, this one bothered me. The image of a man red with blood, cuts and bruises all over his body, and breath so faint that he appeared dead haunted me. It just didn't make sense that people could walk right by him and not help him. There's no way I, or anyone with a heart, could ever do that.

CHAPTER 2

Uncle Roy

Ever since I could remember, my grand-parents had always taken me to church. With my dad being a pilot, and my mom his flight attendant both of my parents were flying a lot. When they were flying, I was always sent to my grandparents' house. I spent more time at their house than my own. Of course, my grandma worried about everything. There were days I couldn't even walk into the living room after school without my grandma asking me a bunch of unnecessary questions.

"Anything I should know about?" she would always ask first.

"Why did it take you so long to get home?" she would ask next.

"Did Tommy invite you over again? I don't think you should be hanging around that kid. I don't like the words that come out of his mouth. When I was younger, I would have had a bar of soap shoved in my mouth for some of those words!" Whenever she got on one of her rants, the words all seemed to blend together. It was one question after another, and of course, I couldn't listen to them all, so I'd end up getting into trouble for ignoring her.

One day, when Grandma was out buying groceries, Grandpa told me she was just concerned about my "well-being" because my parents were gone all the time. Sure, missing my parents hurt me at first, but as a 13-year-old, I thought I was practically a man. I informed Grandpa that I was just too old to be worrying about something like that. After all, I knew my parents loved me.

They were just busy working. Isn't that how all parents are?

To help ease her concern, Grandma always made sure I was in church on Sunday mornings. If I even dared to miss church, I would never hear the end of it. I skipped out just one time...just one time...and it was the worst decision of my young life.

Tommy's older cousin came up one Sunday to hang out with us, so I decided to sneak off to Tommy's house. His cousin always had the funniest stories and the newest toys, and he rarely visited, so I had to hang out with him. I was only going to be gone for a couple of hours, so I didn't think it was a big deal. Man, what a mistake I made. When I got back home, Grandma was sitting very quietly in her rocking chair, just rocking back and forth. That put me on edge right away because she never sat that quietly. I remember her next words as clear as day: "I am so disappointed in you. Your Uncle Roy once snuck off...." I can't remember any words past that. Grandma could yell at me all day, ask me a million questions, or punish me with extra chores, but saying "I am so disappointed" really hurt me. How could I disappoint my Grandma? She did everything for me. And worse, she brought my Uncle Roy into it. I didn't know what Uncle Roy actually did, or where he was at that point, but I knew it wasn't good, and it all started with him deciding to skip a day of church. Grandma always brought that day up and blamed everything he ever did on that one day. All I knew was, I didn't want to be like him. Hearing that I disappointed her, while being compared to Uncle Roy, was something I never wanted to experience again.

CHAPTER 3

Mrs. Porter and "The Good Neighbor"

At church, I always had to be with my Sunday school teacher, Mrs. Porter. Grandma loved to play bingo with Mrs. Porter every Wednesday afternoon. She must have thought since she loved being with Mrs. Porter, that I would too. I thought otherwise. I know she tried to be fun, but she was always so boring. When she told a joke, none of us laughed. Her jokes were so bad, I'm not even sure she knew what a joke was. A blade of grass would make me laugh more than her. I guess with an age gap as large as ours, there just weren't many similarities between us. I couldn't relate to her, and she couldn't relate to me.

During most of Mrs. Porter's lessons, my mind was engaged in other things. I may have had a focusing problem. While she talked about Samson, I thought about my last baseball game. While she talked about David and Goliath, I thought about my next baseball game. While she talked about Daniel, I fell asleep. My mind was always elsewhere. I always thought I had something better to do than to sit in her class and listen. I was only there because of Grandma and Uncle Roy.

But this Sunday was different. This Sunday, I felt angry. I simply could not believe the actions of the two heartless men who had left a lifeless man on the side of a road. After hearing a local news story about two teenagers bullying and robbing a fellow classmate, Mrs. Porter thought it was important for us to learn what it meant to be a good neighbor or a good friend. She always got so worked up over the things going on in our community.

She would always say, "You kids should be as upset about this as I am. After all, this is your world now." She must have thought she wasn't going to live much longer or something.

On this particular Sunday, Mrs. Porter taught us the story about the Good Samaritan. What caught my attention first was this ugly doll she laid on the floor. After looking at the doll carefully, I could make out that it was supposed to be a boy. The doll had red paint all over its body. Its clothes were so torn, I was surprised they were even on the doll. At first, I thought she was just being funny. However, Mrs. Porter's face looked really sad as she pointed her finger at the doll.

"I want you all to imagine that this doll is actually a living, breathing person," she said. "You can clearly see that he is in rough shape. I want you to think about the horrors that this man must have experienced. I want you to feel his pain. I want you to think about what could have happened that would put this man in such a helpless and painful situation."

I had never seen our class so quiet. Normally, Mrs. Porter had to work really hard to keep our class quiet. But on this day, if I had dropped something in the room, it would have sounded like a bomb exploding. Not a single voice could be heard.

Mrs. Porter went on, "As a man was traveling down a road from Jerusalem to Jericho, he was robbed, beaten, and stripped of his clothing. He was just left for dead on the side of the road. Now traveling back then wasn't as easy as it is today. In most cases, people traveled long distances on foot. There weren't police officers to protect you. There weren't even many people traveling the roads. This man just lay there helplessly."

After a short pause, Mrs. Porter continued, "Luckily, a priest happened to be going down the same road." With a concerned look on her face, Mrs. Porter asked, "What do you think the priest did?"

"He's a priest! He obviously helped the man," Corey said.

"You would think so, wouldn't you?" Mrs. Porter replied. "But, he didn't. The priest walked right on by the man."

"What kind of priest would do that?" yelled Corey. "That's terrible!"

"Fortunately, another man happened to be going down the same road," she continued. "However, he didn't stop for the man either."

It was hard to believe that one person could pass someone like him on the road, let alone two people. Our class had such a shock on their faces, it was as if their world had crumbled beneath their feet.

"Finally, a Samaritan, who was also walking down the same road, took pity on the man and decided to help him. He bandaged the man's wounds and helped get him to the nearest town. He even paid the innkeeper in the town to feed and take care of the man when he was gone."

After seeing the relief in our faces, Mrs. Porter asked, "Which man was a better neighbor?"

I normally tried to avoid speaking in the class, but Mrs. Porter had me feeling like a swarm of bees protecting their honey from a bear. I was that worked up!

"The Samaritan," I yelled.

"That's right, Brandon," Mrs. Porter replied. "The Samaritan didn't know the man. He didn't have to stop to help him. He could have walked right on by, too, yet he didn't. The selfless Samaritan showed that he cared about someone he didn't even know."

Mrs. Porter picked up the doll carefully, as if the doll really were a lifeless man.

She said, "You have two choices in your life: you can either choose to be that selfish person who walks on past others in need, or you can choose to be selfless and show that you care for others."

Mrs. Porter put her doll back in her bag, and very quietly, she pulled out her green folder. She always ended every lesson with that silly green folder, so we all knew what to expect. At the end of every lesson, Mrs. Porter would give us a small slip of paper from her folder. She would write down a key word or phrase on each slip that she thought was the most significant piece of the lesson. She hoped it would serve as a reminder for us throughout the week, but most of the time, I just threw my slip away when she wasn't looking. Her "catch phrases" could be so corny or poorly written, I usually thought they weren't even worth keeping. But this lesson had me so worked up, I thought I might need to keep the slip this one time. I thought it might give me some sort of comfort if the image of the helpless man showed up in my head again.

Mrs. Porter quietly, as if to avoid disrupting our thoughts, handed each one of us our little slip. Anxiously, I read it:

"A selfish world is a world full of careless acts, disrespect, and greedy behavior. A selfless world is a world full of love, respect, and passion for others."

CHAPTER 4

Grandma, Grandma, Grandma

Just like in our classroom, the ride home from church was quiet. Grandma must have been really concerned, because instead of asking me her usual list of questions, she tried to distract me. Her way of distracting me was always so random. It was as if she was a dog walking through a park when... "SQUIRREL!!!!!"

"Wow, check out that gorgeous blue car by Johnson's Auto Repair. What do you think of that, Brandon?" Grandma asked. She knew absolutely nothing about cars, so of course she thought since it was so shiny and clean, it must also be special.

"Grandma, that car isn't any better than the car we are sitting in," I murmured.

"How about that new store they are building across the street? What do you think they are going to put in there?" she asked. I'm not sure how she even knew they were putting in a new store. All they had done so far was clear the area. There was nothing more than a flat land of dirt.

"I have no idea, Grandma," I mumbled quietly.

"What do you think about—"

"Honey, stop asking him so many questions," Grandpa interrupted. "Let's leave him alone."

Grandpa always had my back. He'd been married to Grandma for so long that he knew she wouldn't stop asking me questions. I was sure he didn't want to listen to all of her random questions either.

When we finally pulled into our driveway, I remembered that I had my first

baseball practice of the year. I was so dis-
tracted with Mrs. Porter's lesson, I almost
forgot about it. I loved baseball more than
anything, and I could not wait to get on the
field again. I stormed out of the car as fast
as I could, rushed up to my bedroom, and
quickly got dressed. I always wore my favorite pair of black and red shorts, with my
special orange t-shirt. To top it all off, I put
on my old, green baseball hat. I loved the
hat, because there was a really cool buck
logo on the front, and my dad had given it
to me for my birthday when I was six.

"Are you really wearing all of that?"
Grandma asked disappointedly.

"Of course, Grandma, what's wrong with
it?" I replied.

"Everything!" she replied. "I can live
with you looking like a rainbow, but why do
you have to wear that nasty hat?" she asked.
"I love your curly blonde hair!"

I was always terrible at matching my clothes, mainly because I didn't care, but that hat was special to me, and I was going to wear it no matter what.

"Because I like it," I said. "You always tell me that it's what's on the inside that counts." I liked to use things that Grandma had said before to help me in an argument. How could she argue with herself?

"Well, I guess that's true. I'm sure one day your mind will change on that, but I won't rush you. Make sure you come right back after practice," Grandma said.

"I will," I said quickly, as I rushed out of the door as fast as I could. I did not want to give Grandma a chance to ask me any more questions.

CHAPTER 5

The Shortcut

Man, I sure loved baseball! I loved everything about it. I loved the sound from the crack of the bat, the sound of the ball smacking a glove, the sound of someone sliding into a bag, and the sound of the umpire yelling out "Steeeerike three!" (as long as it wasn't to me). Of course, there were also the amazing smells of popcorn, delicious hot dogs, and cotton candy from the concession stand. To top it all off, we always had the best fans to support our team, so we were pumped up to play the game. Our fans would yell special chants for us, bring us food, and do anything they could to show their support. They were the greatest!

I felt that this year was going to be a special year for me. My coach moved me from second base to shortstop, which meant he had a lot of faith in me. As a shortstop, I was going to see so much action and take over as the leader of the team. Because of that, I took every practice seriously. I wanted to make sure I was playing my best every practice so I could play my best every game. I didn't want to make a single error.

As the season approached, with my growing excitement and all of those things weighing heavy on my mind, I couldn't wait to get to practice. Because of how much my grandma worried, she demanded that I always go the same route to the fields.

"I want you to go this route every time. No exceptions," Grandma said to me on my way to my first practice. "The police station is right around the corner, and there are a lot of houses around, so no one is going to do anything crazy," she explained.

However, I felt that as a 13-year-old, I could protect myself. I was also super-fast, so I felt confident that I could outrun any trouble. There was a shortcut to the fields that Tommy had told me about the week before. All I had to do was take a left at the first traffic light and go through two alleys. It cut off at least a half a mile of walking. I would go through it so quickly; nothing could go wrong. Besides, Grandma had no way of finding out.

As I made my left turn to head down the first alleyway, I hoped that with all the time I was saving, I'd be able to get a few extra grounders in with the coach before the rest of the team got there. The coach was always there way before us, so I knew the earlier I got there, the better. I really wanted to show him that I was ready to go and could handle the new challenge. I was halfway through the alley, walking past an old beat-up dumpster, when a strange-looking pile of something caught my attention. I couldn't tell at first what I was looking at. It just looked like dirty, torn-up clothes. I was about to keep walking when I saw the mound move, like it had its own little pulse. Thinking about what my grandma had said, I was a little worried that she might be right. Was I about to experience this "crazy" she was talking about? I wasn't sure what to think, but I decided to creep closer towards the mound to get a better look.

I couldn't believe my eyes. It was a young boy! His clothes looked horrible. They were so dirty and full of holes that they really weren't serving any purpose. It looked like he had red and purple marks all over his face. And as I checked him over closer, I noticed he had them all over his arms and legs, too, but what would have caused that? He was so unrecognizable, that I couldn't even tell what color hair he had. I was at a loss for words and had no idea what to do. I so badly wanted to get to my baseball practice, but if I tried to help this boy out, I knew I might miss it. So many thoughts were swirling around in my head. What would Coach Carter do if I missed practice? I was terrified that he would think I wasn't dedicated enough and that he would send me back to second base, or even worse: What if he cut me? I wouldn't be able to live without baseball. Baseball was my life.

With all these thoughts swarming through my mind, I decided there had to be someone walking down the street with more time than me. They could certainly help this boy out. I figured all I had to do was yell for him, since he clearly couldn't speak for himself. Without wasting any more time, I slammed my hand against the dumpster as hard as I could, and yelled, "Help! Help!" Dumpsters are so loud; I figured the racket had to alarm someone out there. Just to make sure he got the help he needed, I slammed my hand against the dumpster again and yelled "Help!" one more time.

I was sure he'd be okay. I had been so loud, there was no way I wouldn't have been heard by somebody.

CHAPTER 6

The Perfect Practice

You know that feeling on Christmas morning when you wake up at the crack of dawn, full of excitement? You can't wait to run to the living room with your family and open that first, much-anticipated present. That's how I felt when I arrived at the baseball fields and saw Coach Carter waiting anxiously in the dugout. I was so stoked about starting baseball that when I rounded the last corner, I sprinted to the fields.

"Hey, Coach Carter!" I yelled. "I can't believe baseball season is finally here!"

"Hey, Brandon, I've been waiting a long time for this season as well," he replied.

"You were so excited you had to come smell the field early, huh?"

"Actually, I wanted to ask you if you could hit me some grounders, so I can start working on my game," I said.

Being at shortstop meant I was going to be getting a lot of ground balls and hard liners hit my way. I wanted to get every bit of practice I could.

"Absolutely!" he responded. "I love a kid who wants to put in the extra time."

Knowing that I had about 20 minutes before the rest of the team would show up, I took full advantage of my one-on-one time with my coach. It was a blast! He started off hitting me slow, easy grounders to build my confidence, but by the time the rest of the boys were showing up, he was cranking those baseballs at me. The last one he hit was a line drive that hit the ground just short of my legs, which are always tough to dig up. I picked it up so naturally, I felt like I could step in for a shortstop in the major leagues. My confidence was flying high.

"What a play!" Tommy yelled at me with excitement. "It's going to be awesome having you back there this year. It'll be hard for any team to get hits against us."

"With you pitching, and Corey on third, they better hope we have some off days," I replied.

We really did have a strong team. Corey was one of the best infielders I had ever seen. I couldn't remember the last time he let one go by him. At first base, we had Kyler. Though he was a goofy, slightly awkward kid, he was tall and lanky, and would stop any bad throw that came his way. At first base, you have to make sure you catch that ball and get the out, no matter how poorly the ball is thrown. And in the outfield, we had three boys who were faster than anyone in our league. They could absolutely fly to the ball. On top of that, those boys could catch any ball hit to them. It was almost as if they put super glue in their gloves. I don't know if I ever saw them drop a ball.

The excitement and pure joy of being on this team was evident on everyone's face. I could tell everyone knew what kind of team we had, and we all had big dreams for this year. Boys were flying to the ball as it flew off the bat, running hard around the bases and even cheering when coach had us do some extra running to get into shape, which I'd never seen. I mean, how many kids really want to run for no reason? It was the best first practice I'd ever been a part of.

As practice came to a close, Coach called us all in for our usual quick talk and team breakdown. "That was an outstanding practice, boys!" he said. "I am really excited to see what's in store for us this year. Let's make sure we stay focused and continue to work as hard as we did today."

It was almost as if Coach Carter was afraid we would have some sort of fallout after this practice, but I wasn't concerned about it at all. We looked way too good to fail.

"Brandon, will you break it down for us?" he asked.

I was blown away. Coach Carter only asked his most trusted athletes to break it down after a practice. In fact, no one on our team had ever been called on to do it, so to say I was excited and honored was an understatement. I was so shocked, I nearly forgot what our team mascot was.

"Let's go!" I yelled. "Lions on three: One...two...three..."

"Lions!" everyone yelled.

I'm pretty sure people all across the world heard us yell. It was the purest sound

I'd ever heard, which of course, just added to our excitement.

Before picking up my backpack to walk home, I heard an unexpected voice calling for me.

"Brandon!" Grandma yelled. "Over here!"

It was unusual for Grandma to pick me up after a practice, but with how hard I worked, I was relieved to have a ride home. I was beyond exhausted, and I couldn't wait for my head to touch my pillow. I was expecting a lot of questions, as usual, but she really surprised me. She was as quiet as the woods on a cold crisp morning. So quiet in fact that I was on the edge of my seat the whole way home. I thought for sure she found out I had taken that shortcut, but how in the world would she have known? I know no one saw me because I double-checked the street before entering the alley, and when I left the alley to get to the fields, there wasn't anyone in sight. But I still felt that something wasn't right.

When we finally arrived home, we both walked into the house calmly, as if nothing was going on. Did she really have nothing to ask me? I was in awe. She clearly knew nothing about my shortcut and had no questions for me. I figured I was in the clear to use that shortcut again and planned on using it from then on.

With so much confidence in myself, I rushed up to the bathroom, showered, brushed my teeth, and jumped right into my bed. Whenever you work hard, that feeling of falling into your soft, comfortable bed is probably one of the best feelings ever. I thought for sure I would fall asleep immediately, but when I rolled over, I noticed a crumpled-up slip of paper sitting there on my pillow. I knew I hadn't put anything on my pillow, because earlier that day, I was only in my room for a few minutes. I looked around the room and noticed a few of my things were out of place, and there was a big heap of clean clothes on my dresser. That was definitely not from me. If there was a list of the most unorganized people in this world, I believe I'd be at the top of that list. This was clearly Grandma. My grandma loved to spend as much time with me as she could, so she liked to do the laundry when I was gone. She must have brought me my laundry while I was at practice.

Suddenly, I had this lonely, empty, aching feeling in the pit of my stomach. It was as if I had been hit by a train. I realized that the slip of paper on my pillow was Mrs. Porter's message from earlier that day— the message that had gotten me all worked up. I had completely forgotten about it since all I could focus on earlier was baseball. Grandma must have found it in my pair of shorts and put it on my pillow.

"But how could they?" I asked. "How could they walk right by him?"

"That's a great question Brandon," Mrs. Porter had replied. "Maybe they were late for something. Maybe they thought they had something more important to do. Or maybe they just thought, surely someone else would take care of it. After all, they didn't even know the man."

My conversation with Mrs. Porter earlier that day burned in my head over and over again. It just replayed in my head. I couldn't believe anyone would walk by someone who was clearly hurting. But hadn't I just done that early in the day?! Had I really done that, too?! I was sure someone had gotten to that boy. There's no way they couldn't have. I mean, I did hit that dumpster as loud as I could, and my voice carries far, so I knew someone heard me yell. But still...how could I have done that? I could see his face full of agony, and it bothered me. I couldn't believe what I had done. I opened the crumpled-up slip of paper, and reread her message:

"A selfish world is a world full of careless acts, disrespect, and greedy behavior. A selfless world is a world full of love, respect, and passion for others."

CHAPTER 7

What a Dream

My eyes were getting heavier and heavier as I knew my exhaustion was about to take me into a deep sleep, but her words...those burning words. I couldn't seem to get them out of my head. As my eyes closed, I started to feel strange. It was as if some strange force was tugging at me, pulling me into a dream. An unreal chill crept over me, so I tried to grab my blanket to cover me up, but my blanket was gone. I reached all over for it, but it was nowhere to be found. Confusion began to overwhelm me when I noticed my room was missing more than just my blanket. In fact, the only thing I saw besides the bed I was on was a very large, bright yellow door in front of me. Nothing was making any sense. How in the world did I end up there? Whenever I'm half-asleep, things don't seem to make sense, but that yellow door really confused me. I started to wonder if maybe Grandma painted my door yellow while I was at practice, but there was no reason for her to waste her time doing that, and that didn't explain why everything else was missing.

Cautiously, I crept toward the yellow door, knowing it was my only escape. I hoped that whatever was behind the door would clear my mind and take me back to reality, but it was just the opposite. As I opened the door, voices thundered through the opening. They were so loud, it terrified me. I slammed the door so quickly; I didn't even realize that I had done it. I'd never heard voices that deafening. Thousands of people had to be there to make such an intense sound.

Lifeless

Nothing made any sense. I didn't want to reopen the door, but there was nowhere else for me to go. Reluctantly, I opened the door again. Once again, that same insane volume of voices overwhelmed my ears. As I stepped forward, I saw there were thousands of people staring at me, with unexpected smiles on their faces. You could see so much joy in their eyes. I had no idea what they were smiling about, but it kind of took that unsettling feeling away from me at that moment. As I looked around, I noticed that ahead of me was one very long aisle, which was only about five feet wide. The aisle seemed to go on for miles. There was no way for me to see the end of it. On both sides of the aisle were thousands of people sitting in stadium seats. I realized I was in some sort of weird stadium. Although I watch a lot of sports, I'd never seen a stadium like this one. Its layout didn't make any sense. Why would people surround a five-foot-wide aisle? There couldn't possibly be anything exciting to watch.

As I stood there, just staring down the aisle, not knowing what to expect, my ears slowly cleared up. I was able to make out what the people were chanting at me:

"A selfless world is a world full of love, respect, and passion for others."

Even with thousands of people chanting, I could hear it so clearly. Each person said each word at the exact same time. Not a single person was behind or ahead of the next, and they just kept repeating it over and over again. It reminded me of an ocean's wave flowing forcefully upon a shore then receding just as powerfully.

"A selfless world is a world full of love, respect, and passion for others."

At first, I thought, why are they only saying the second sentence of Mrs. Porter's message? But then I thought, wait a minute, why are they saying it at all?

"Hey, sir!" I yelled to a man in the front row. "Where am I? What's going on?" I could feel a little panic coming back as it all started to overwhelm me again. The man, like the rest of "my fans" in the stadium, didn't skip a beat. He continued chanting the same phrase repeatedly. Though he was looking at me, it felt more like he was just looking through me.

Knowing the door behind me had nothing for me, I decided I'd better walk down the aisle to see if anything good was ahead. I walked for what felt like hours. My feet began to ache, and I could feel myself walking more slowly by the minute. I noticed I had gotten so used to the voices, I hardly even heard them anymore. Step after step, hour after hour, I kept walking forward, but I still couldn't see an end. If you've ever done something boring before, whether it was some sort of job or a school project, you know how redundant things can get. In fact, you probably did that job or project without hardly paying attention to what was going on around you. That's what it was like for me. I was walking so long that I didn't realize all the changes going on around me.

Finally, after what seemed like years, I saw another door at the end of the aisle. It appeared to be the exact same door as the one I had left earlier. The size and shape were identical, only the color was different. It was red. A strange feeling of excitement overcame me, as I felt I was finally nearing the end of whatever this was, until I looked back at the crowd of people. I realized that I hadn't looked back at them for quite a while. Their faces had completely changed—it terrified me! I looked at as many faces as I could, hoping to see just one person who looked happy, but not a single person showed any hint of a smile. Every-one's eyes looked like they were soaked with tears, and their lips were turned over in one of the saddest frowns I'd ever seen. Whether they had just lost a job, lost someone close to them, or had some other terrible experience, seeing thousands of sad, depressed, and hurt people is a feeling I just can't describe. I had to close my eyes to clear my mind of their faces, but it made things even worse. Not only had their faces changed, but their words had also. Their constant chanting was still in sync, but their message was different. Over and over again, I heard:

"A selfish world is a world full of careless acts, disrespect, and greedy behavior."

When I heard what they were saying, I knew something drastic was changing. I had to get out of there. Without even thinking about what was behind it, I opened the red door and stepped inside as fast as I could.

"A selfish world—" SLAM!

CHAPTER 8

A Changed World

When I was a lot younger, nightmares were a frequent thing for me. I remember going through a phase where grizzly bears absolutely terrified me, and it seemed like all the movies I watched with my family had grizzly bears in them. I would have dreams where the bears were chasing me, and of course, no matter how hard I tried to run, I wouldn't get anywhere. I even had a dream once when I was in math class at school, where a massive grizzly bear barged through our classroom door and attacked me. After my grizzly bear phase came the falling from steep places phase. I would randomly have dreams where I was falling from things like houses, towers, or even mountains. The worst part of the dream was the split second before impacting the ground. At that point, I'd feel like my life was about to be over. It scared me so badly that it would completely shake me out of my sleep. Trembling and sweaty, it took me hours to settle back down. I had such a hard time falling back to sleep that sometimes it took me days to get over that dream.

But I can't remember the last time I had a nightmare. That was, until this day. It was unusual for me to even remember a dream anymore, yet this was one I could remember vividly. I was able to remember every little detail, from the faces of the people in the crowd, to the colors of the tiles along the aisle floor. I knew something wasn't right with that dream, but I tried to get it out of my head. I figured, like every other nightmare I had as a kid, that in time this one would fade away and leave me alone. I couldn't have been more wrong.

At first, I was feeling much better. Everything around my room was right back to where it should be, and there was no strange yellow or red door in front of me, which was great.

The day before, while at practice, Tommy and I had talked about going to the fair. We were probably getting a little old for the rides, but even though we wouldn't admit it to others, we still enjoyed them. We'd gone to the fair ever since I could remember. It felt like a tradition.

Since going to the fair was a special occasion for us, I grabbed my special tennis shoes. Before my parents had left on a work trip a couple months ago, they bought me the newest pair of Nikes you could get. I loved them so much that I didn't want to scuff them, so I hardly ever wore them. In fact, I probably only wore them a couple of times since I got them, but as I said, this was a special occasion that called for some style. I even put on a nice blue polo shirt and my best khaki shorts.

"Grandma!" I yelled as I walked down the stairs. "I am headed to the fair to meet up with Tommy."

If I ever left the house without telling Grandma, I'd be in major trouble, so I had to make sure she knew I was going out. It was pretty common for her to miss what I was saying. Her hearing obviously wasn't quite as good as it used to be, but you can't expect someone as old as her to hear that well. I mean, 80 years of sound has hit her ear drums, and I have no idea what kind of sounds those might have been.

I checked everywhere for Grandma, but she was nowhere to be found. It wasn't like her or Grandpa to leave without waking me up and telling me. Usually, she had a big plan for the day, and if I was left at home alone, I was given directions for something, even for simple things, like how to wash my hands properly.

"Grandma...Grandpa?" I kept yelling, "Where are you guys?"

The house was so silent, you could hear a feather hit the floor. I kept pacing through the house, trying to see if they had left me anything. I didn't want to get into trouble for leaving, but I wasn't sure how to let her know where I was going if I couldn't find her. After searching all over the house, I finally found what appeared to be a little note. Normally, Grandma would write as clearly as possible for me so there was no excuse for me to miss something, but this note was so small and there was hardly anything written on it. All it said was:

Grandpa and I are taking a trip to California. We will be gone for a couple of months.

Love, Grandma

Was this a joke? There's no way she was serious. Grandma was such a worrywart. How could she expect me to make it without her for that long? My parents weren't even going to be home for another three weeks, so what was I supposed to do? I was feeling a little angry that Grandma would do that to me. It seemed selfish of her, and it didn't seem like something Grandma would actually do. As I thought about it more, I began to laugh. Grandpa had clearly written that note as a joke. There was no other explanation that would make sense.

As a 13-year-old, I knew I could handle anything, so I left the house. If Grandma didn't want to tell me what was really going on, I figured it didn't matter if I left. As soon as I stepped out of the house, I smelled something so raunchy, it made me gag. I didn't know what I was smelling, but whatever it was, it had to be close. Our street was always so clean because my grandma felt that this street represented us. She hated the thought of what people would think if they saw even one tiny piece of paper in the street. She even got our neighbors to be on the same page. Everyone in our neighborhood was responsible for picking up in front of their house, whether that was their yard, the sidewalk, or the road. Yet the smells around my neighborhood were unreal. And worse, there was trash everywhere. Trash was on everyone's yard, all over the sidewalks, and on the roads. The roads were so dirty that I figured cars would have a hard time driving.

I hoped that some kid was just playing a prank on our neighborhood, but as I walked down the street to go meet Tommy, I noticed that every road, alley, parking lot, and yard looked the same: trashed, dirty, broken.

I turned the corner and noticed even Mr. Jones's flower shop was messed up. He was always so particular about his shop. Normally, beautiful flowers lined the front of his building, and he washed his windows so often that it was impossible to see even a hint of dust. People loved to drive through this part of town, just to see his beautiful shop. Yet on this day, his windows were so dirty you couldn't see through them. This was more unusual and puzzling than anything I had ever seen.

I went into his shop to find out what was going on. When I saw him, he wasn't his usual happy self. He seemed down, as if he had lost someone close to him. Even on his worst days, Mr. Jones always had a smile on his face. He once told me that if you're having a bad day but still hold a smile, you can lift yourself up and help other people feel good about themselves—all with a simple smile. I loved going to see him for that reason, and it really helped me do the same for others.

"Hey, Mr. Jones, how are you?" I asked.

"I'm surviving. What do you need?" he replied.

"I don't need anything. I was kind of concerned about you when I saw your windows. Did something happen?" I asked.

"What's wrong with my windows?!" he snapped at me. The way he said it really concerned me. I'd never seen him act like that before.

"I just noticed they were a little dirty is all, but if it doesn't matter to you, I guess it's not a big deal to me either," I said.

"Don't you have better things to worry about than my windows?" he replied. "I don't have time to worry about them, and I don't care what people think when they see my windows."

Speechless, I just walked out of his building. I began to wonder if he had some sort of strange accident. When I walked back outside and saw everyone's faces, I realized that my whole town must have had that same weird accident. Everyone seemed sad and serious. What was going on?

"Hey, excuse me!" I heard a voice yell. I turned to look and was shocked. An older woman was knocked completely over by a younger man. It was obvious that she was in pain from her fall. It looked like she had hit her head hard, because she immediately put her hand on her forehead. She then tried to get up but fell right back down and cried in pain as she held her fragile knee. The man didn't hardly even look at her.

"You need to pay attention to where you're walking!" he yelled back at her.

"Please, sir, can you help me up?" she begged. "I hurt my knee."

Without hesitating, the young man took off. He never looked back or showed any evidence of questioning his decision to walk away. I couldn't believe someone could be so selfish, especially when he was the reason she was hurt in the first place. Even worse than that was the fact that no one was stopping to help her. They were just walking by as well, as if they were more important than her.

I knew I needed to help her, but as I began to walk towards her to help, I felt a strong, firm hand grip my arm. There was so much pressure on my arm, I could feel it turning numb.

"How in the world did you get those shoes?" a boy asked me, pointing at my new Nikes.

"My parents gave them to me," I replied.

"Ha, yeah right," he laughed. "No one wears shoes like those around here. Who'd you steal them from?"

"I didn't steal them from anyone. Like I said, my parents gave them to me," I said.

"Well, you're going to have to give those to me. Those shoes are clearly too nice for you, and I need the money," he said aggressively, as he squeezed my arm tighter. "I could easily get a hundred bucks for those shoes," he said.

"I'm not giving you my shoes. What is wrong with you?" I asked.

"What did you say to me?" he asked. He put his face right up to mine, where his nose just barely missed mine. Shock began to overtake me again. I don't like confrontation, and I had never been in a fight. I could tell this boy meant business. I knew I better listen to him, or I was going to get myself hurt.

"Listen, kid, I don't know who you think you are, but I'm taking these shoes no matter what. You can either hand them to me without getting hurt, or I'll take them from you," he said. "You're not going to like the second option," he warned.

Lifeless

Not knowing what else to do, I bent over to untie my shoes and quickly gave them to him. So many thoughts swirled in my mind as he ran off with my shoes. I was afraid my parents would be mad at me for losing my new shoes. But even more concerning was the alarming amount of horrible behavior going on around me. Between Mr. Jones yelling at me, a woman being shoved down in the street, and my shoes being stolen from me, it seemed that my world had completely changed. Everything seemed out of control. Before this day, the only bad thing I ever saw in our neighborhood was when Terry's dog pooped in Mrs. Miller's Garden. Anyone in the neighborhood would have offered to help. Yet on this day, there was no one to go to for help. There were no police officers to be seen, no people in the streets offering to help each other, and not a single person who seemed to even care about anyone but themselves. It seemed my world had taken a turn for the worse.

I no longer had any interest in trying to go to the fair with Tommy, and to be honest, I was starting to doubt I'd be able to find him anyway with the way things were going. My heart felt broken and overwhelmed with what I was seeing. As I trudged back home, I tried to avoid watching people. I just couldn't bear to see another incident going on in the street, and I couldn't get that woman in the street off my mind. I truly felt lost.

Sitting in my silent house, I realized my grandpa and grandma were not playing a prank on me. They really had left me at home by myself. I couldn't believe it! I sat down on my couch and rested my head on the arm, trying to figure out what I should do next. One thing was for sure, I definitely did not want to leave my house again.

CHAPTER 9

Left with Nothing

The next day, I was feeling way more optimistic. That was, until I opened the fridge. I was so hungry; I could've eaten anything. With all that I saw and felt the day before, I realized I hadn't eaten a single thing. I rushed to the fridge to make myself my favorite sandwich, ham and cheese. But the fridge was almost empty. Other than a jar of pickles and some leftover spaghetti, there wasn't anything to eat. I checked the cupboards by the fridge where we normally stored our cookies and chips, and it also was empty. The pantry was no different. Even the cans of ravioli, which we never ate, were gone from the pantry.

My next thought was to find some money. If we didn't have food in the fridge, I could at least go buy something to eat. One of my favorite things to do was walk down the street to the corner gas station to buy myself some treats, usually a bag of candy and a can of pop. My grandparents always trusted me to walk down there on my own. Near that gas station was the grocery store, which I knew I needed immediately. Grandpa always stored some extra cash in a metal container in their top dresser drawer. However, like the other disappointments, their drawer was completely empty as well. I don't know if I'd ever felt so hopeless. No food. No money. I knew I could talk a big game for only being a 13-year-old, but I really didn't know what to do. I wasn't prepared to be alone, and I had no idea how I was going to get what I needed.

Lifeless

After scarfing down the pickles and what was left of the spaghetti, I knew I had to do something about my situation. I went upstairs to get myself dressed for the day. Instead of wearing nice clothes, I thought that it might be best to wear some of my worn-out clothes. I didn't want a replay of what happened the day before, so I chose clothes that wouldn't make me stand out. They were stained and faded, which I was sure no one would ever want. Since my new shoes were gone, my only other option were my old tennis shoes, which had multiple holes in them and looked to be as old as I was. I definitely wasn't going to have a problem with some punk kid stealing my shoes again.

Remembering everything I saw the day before, I tried to avoid people on the street. I did not want to make eye contact, which wasn't too difficult, since it seemed that nobody else wanted to either. People clearly didn't care at all about anyone but themselves. It was like they didn't know other people even existed. But it was impossible not to notice all the filth and the stench coming from the streets. I saw building after building that used to be so beautiful, yet they were clearly not taken care of anymore. I walked faster and faster, until I realized my walk had turned into a run. I decided I needed to check up on Tommy. I thought maybe he could clear some things up for me, but at the same time, I was worried that maybe he was in worse shape than I was.

Tommy's house was only five blocks away from my house, so he and I would go back and forth to each other's houses all the time. Grandma never had a problem with it because we were always on the main streets, which to her, were safe. I'm glad she wasn't around to see the changes I was seeing, though. I don't think she would have even let me step outside of the house.

I was so excited when I arrived at Tommy's house. It felt like it had been forever since I was able to talk with someone I knew, and all the sadness in people's faces was really wearing on me. To not see a single happy person is an eerie feeling. Normally, even when people are having a bad day, there is someone you can count on who won't let it get them down. When I got to Tommy's front door, instead of knocking like I normally would, I stormed right through.

"Tommy! You here?" I yelled. "Tommy!"

"I'm in the living room," I heard a voice reply back.

Without hesitating, I went into the living room. So thankful to see a familiar face, I rushed up to Tommy. But as soon as I saw him, that discouraging, gut-wrenching feeling overcame me again.

Tommy didn't look the same either. He was so dirty. It didn't look like he had showered in weeks, and he looked exhausted. His eyes were so droopy that he must not have slept in quite a while.

"What's going on, Tommy?" I asked him.

"I'm just getting ready for work," he replied.

Tommy had always been one of the laziest kids I'd ever met. I thought he was joking when he said he was going to work. That absolutely was not like him.

"Yeah right," I laughed. "Why would you need to go to work?"

Tommy's parents always spoiled him, which is probably why he was so lazy in the first place. He always seemed to get what he wanted, no matter what it was. I really did think he was joking about working.

"My parents left me by myself," he said sadly. "They said they wanted to travel around the world, and that I was just going to hold them back."

I could see tears flowing down his face, which I completely understood. I could see the same lost feeling in his face that I'd been experiencing.

"They didn't leave me anything," he continued. "I had to get a job at the factory just to make some money so I could put food on the table."

"Wow, Tommy, I'm sorry to hear that," I replied. I didn't want him to know that I was in the same situation because I didn't want him to worry about me. He and I had been close friends for years, so we always helped each other out as much as we could. There was no need to make him feel any worse than he already did, and besides, I wasn't sure what I should do either. A wave of disbelief came over me as I thought about the changes that had suddenly taken place. It sure seemed like a lot for a couple of 13-year-olds whose biggest trouble a year ago was deciding whether to eat Fruit Loops or Cheerios for breakfast.

Have you ever watched a sloth move through the trees in the Amazon? Then you can understand what I was seeing when Tommy stood up. As he began to stand up, he hunched his body over his legs and grabbed hold of the couch to help push himself up. I wasn't sure if he was going to move from that position, because he didn't try to stand up for quite some time. With a moan, he finally mustered up the strength to stand and began to slowly head for the door.

"We'll have to catch up some other time, Brandon," he said. "It's back to the grind for me."

"Just do me a favor when you get back home, Tommy," I replied. "Make sure you get some sleep. You're not looking so good."

"I try to get sleep, but my boss changes my hours all the time," he said. "He doesn't care how we're feeling or what's going on."

"What do you mean?" I asked.

"All he cares about is getting his money. I worked a 12-hour shift just four hours ago, yet he already called me back for another one," Tommy said.

"Why don't you work somewhere else then?" I asked.

"They're all the same," he replied. "And if you don't do what they say, they fire you. I won't survive without the money. I don't have a choice."

Tommy turned around, grabbed a little bag with some food, and opened the door to leave. Right before he closed the door, without even using the energy to turn to face me, he said, "Good luck, Brandon. I hope things are working out better for you."

CHAPTER 10

Job Search

To say I was even more lost would be an understatement. Seeing the way Tommy was struggling made me extremely nervous. I'd never had a job, other than cleaning my room and occasionally doing the dishes when Grandma made me. I didn't know of any 13-year-old who was ready to work like an adult, but I knew I needed to find a job, too. There wasn't anyone to support me at home, and I didn't have any money at all. I couldn't buy food, clothes, or even toilet paper, and what if my parents or grandparents weren't coming back? I would never have worried about that before, but I also never would've worried about Mr. Jones's windows, or the streets, or the way people treated each other; yet now I was. This was not the world I was used to. If they never showed back up, then our bills wouldn't be paid either. No lights, no heat, no house!

Finding a job became my top priority and my top concern. What if Tommy was right? Was every boss going to be the same? Maybe Tommy just didn't look in the right places. The more I thought about it, I figured I'd have a better chance getting away from the factories. I knew there was a large farm straight west of my house. There weren't a lot of farms in the area, so this one was huge and had to do a lot. I grimly thought it might be better to work with animals than with some of the people I'd met so far.

The farm was at least a two-mile walk for me because I obviously didn't have a car and couldn't drive, but that didn't scare me. I figured it was probably better to get away from the city anyway. After all, how much worse could it get? At the very least, there would be fewer people to encounter and worry about.

Boy, what a terrible walk it was. As I got closer to the farm, I saw that the houses, stores, and people were all still the same. Broken windows were everywhere. There was trash and filth as far as the eye could see, people shoving other people, and strangers yelling at complete strangers for even the smallest things. I think I even witnessed five different thefts, and no one was there to help. I knew there was no way I could jump in to help someone. What's a 13-year-old going to do to people double his size? Three out of the five thefts were for pairs of shoes. It seemed that anyone wearing nice shoes was bound to lose them, unless you were tough enough to fight for them. The other two thefts were men stealing purses from older ladies. There were people all over the streets, yet no one cared enough to help them. They just kept minding their own business.

I guess it was a good thing I wasn't carrying anything valuable with me, but then I began to worry about how I was going to keep my money when I got paid. If someone attacked me to take my money, there wasn't much I could do. I knew I'd have to find some sort of special place to store my money, and also move quickly to avoid the risk of being robbed. No one was going to take my hard-earned cash away from me. I didn't care who they were.

When I approached the farm, I realized how big it really was. There had to be a job for me there. I could see horses, sheep, and cows right out front, grazing in their pastures. There were so many, you could smell their stench from a mile away. I knew the farmer would need a lot of people to help run a massive farm like that, so I wasn't too concerned about getting a job.

I finally made it to the driveway of the farm and began walking towards what looked like the farmer's office. Before getting there, I saw a young, grubby kid walking towards me. I should probably rephrase that. I smelled a young, grubby kid walking towards me. Man, did he smell awful. I sure didn't want whatever job he had. I didn't think a shower would even come close to curing whatever was coming off of him.

"Hey there, how are ya?" I asked. I made sure to smile, since no one else seemed to do that, hoping I could get a smile out of someone.

"Good luck," he replied, without even looking at me. His facial expression never changed at all, not even a little bit. At first, I couldn't get over how rude he was, but I guess I was getting kind of used to that. He sure made me feel uncomfortable though. Maybe things weren't better over here, like I thought. Maybe Tommy was right, and all bosses were the same.

The old front door of the farmer's office was so loud, I thought for sure it would scare him when I opened it. He didn't jump, twitch, or even move. In fact, he didn't look at me at all. Man, I thought, is there really no one out there who can treat another person respectfully? Where are people's manners? There was absolutely no way he didn't hear the door, yet he didn't seem to care as I entered.

"Hello, sir, my name is Brandon," I began. "I was wondering if you had any jobs available."

"That depends," he responded. "How hard are you willing to work? You look a little small, and we have a lot of work to do on this farm." This was the first time he paid any attention to me, as he scanned me over. Since I now affected his work, he must have thought I was important to him.

"I'll work as hard as you need, sir," I said.

"Well, it's your lucky day then. I just fired a kid, so you can take his job," he said. "I will pay you seven bucks an hour, and I expect you to be here whenever I tell you." After listening to Tommy's story, I knew what that meant. He was intending on working me as long and as hard as possible.

"Thank you, sir," I responded. I knew I didn't have any other option. "When do you need me to work?" I asked.

"Right now," he said, turning to the closed door right behind him. "Jimmy! I need you out here," he yelled. A tall, skinny kid, probably near my age, emerged from the back room. He looked a little like the farmer, so I figured he was probably one of his kids, and man did he look clean. I thought everyone would be dirty from all their work around the farm, but it looked like Jimmy hadn't worked a day in his life. I guess it's not a bad life when your dad's the boss.

"Jimmy, I want you to take Brandon around the farm to tell him what he's going to do. I just fired Joey, so he'll be doing his job."

"Alright, Dad," Jimmy said. He looked me over and laughed. I'm sure his laugh wasn't a good thing, but at least I finally found someone who didn't look so angry. He waved his hand at me, which I assumed was his way of telling me to follow him, so I stood up and acted like I knew what I was doing. I hoped my confidence would take that smirk off his face.

Before hardly even stepping out of the office, I heard Jimmy mumble something, and again, I saw him laugh.

"What'd you say?" I asked, hoping it was something good.

"I said you'll be lucky if you make a week. I've never seen such a small worker on our farm." He laughed again.

"I'll be fine. Just show me what I need to do," I said. I was getting sick of everyone's attitude, and even though he didn't look angry, his laugh was almost worse.

As Jimmy took me around the farm, I realized how massive the place actually was. I never would have thought a farm could have so many animals, but this farm had way more than you could ever try to count. I'm sure it was very difficult to keep track of all of them. There were thousands of cows in the biggest barn I'd ever seen, a large pasture for their sheep, and an equally large pasture for their horses.

Finally, Jimmy took me to the pig barn. The barn wasn't quite as big as the cow barn, but it held even more pigs. There were so many rooms filled with pigs crammed so tightly they could hardly move. Jimmy explained to me that they had the pigs in the different rooms, based on their age. I learned quickly how aggressive pigs could be and how important it was to monitor where pigs were placed, and which pigs they were placed with. In the middle of the barn, there were even more pigs. These pigs were tightly packed in their own special stall, but with how fast Jimmy was walking, I couldn't ask him why these pigs were separated. The overall size of the farm was so massive, and his careless attitude made me think that he was getting tired of explaining things to me. However, he made it clear what my job was, and it was not exciting. Not exciting at all. I was expected to clean the rooms, the stalls, the aisles, and pretty much anything else around these pigs. With so many pigs in such a large area, the farm had to hire multiple people just to clean. I wasn't going to do anything else but clean all day.

Lifeless

And clean I did—12 hours of just sweeping, scooping, and scrubbing all day. My fingers and hands were so raw by the end of the day that I couldn't move them at all. The pulse from my heartbeat could be felt throughout my hands, and boy was that painful. I was so relieved to be done that I almost forgot to ask the farmer when I was needed next before heading home. I knew from Tommy that if I didn't get there when he wanted, I wouldn't be keeping my job.

Exhausted and sore, I headed to the farmer. I wanted to find him quickly so I could get home and go right to bed, but of course, I couldn't find him anywhere. The distance between buildings and the size of the farm made finding him impossible. For all I knew, we could've just been walking away from each other the whole time. When I went to the cow barn, he could've been headed to the sheep pasture, and when I went there, he could've gone into the horse barn.

After about a half hour of searching, I ran into Jimmy, who I was sure would also be able to tell me what time I was needed.

"You made it through your first day, huh?" Jimmy said.

"Yeah, it wasn't too bad," I lied.

"Well, your hands are telling me a different story," he said, grabbing ahold of my hands. "You better take care of these tonight. If dad sees you slowing down, you won't be here much longer."

"I'll be fine," I said confidently. "Do you know what time I need to be back tomorrow?" I asked. I was really hoping I'd be able to get a lot of sleep, but since it was already midnight, I was concerned about how much I could really get.

"Pig barns don't clean themselves," he said laughing like earlier. "We need you back here at 4:00 in the morning."

"Are you serious?!" I asked, completely shocked. Inside, I knew he was serious, but I had to ask. How could I do this if I had to be back at 4:00? Between walking the two miles back home, and walking the two miles back to work, I knew I wouldn't get more than a couple of hours of sleep, if that.

"Of course I am," he said. I could tell he wasn't happy that I had asked him that. His whole demeanor changed. "Is that going to be a problem?" he asked me.

I was so exhausted and discouraged from my day, I just wanted to go home. Slouched over, with my head down, I responded, "No it won't be. I'll be back tomorrow."

Without exchanging any more words, Jimmy pulled out some cash and handed it to me for my day's work. As promised, I was paid seven dollars an hour. Though it didn't seem like much, I was thankful I had some cash. Besides the pickles and leftover spaghetti, I hadn't eaten all day, and I now had a way to get myself some food.

To protect my money from other people, I tucked the money inside my sock. I didn't think anyone would search for my money there. Then, with the little bit of energy I had left, I ran home.

CHAPTER 11

Over and Over Again

Cleaning, cleaning, cleaning.... That's all I ever did. It seemed my life was flashing before my eyes. No more bike rides with Tommy, no more strolls through the park with my grandparents, and worst of all, no more baseball. Man was I missing baseball. The farmer had me working almost nonstop. I barely had a break to even stop and eat or to use the bathroom. I can remember so clearly what Tommy looked like when I went to his house to check on him, and there was no doubt in my mind that I began to look the same way. I was flat-out exhausted and clearly overworked, and I had little opportunity to sleep. I sure could've used a two- or three-day nap.

Though my hands had gotten used to all the abuse, I felt my body getting weaker and weaker every day. It's so difficult for your body to recover from all the hours of work when you can't get enough sleep. And to make matters worse, on just my second day on the job, I was bitten so badly by one of the boars, it was painful to do just about anything. I knew I needed to be careful around Jimmy and his dad because they would fire me on the spot if I looked slow, so I continued to push through as if I wasn't injured at all.

My job became really discouraging. It seemed like everything I did was for nothing. As soon as I'd clean a room or a stall, it was nasty again within the hour. It got so bad at times that I would occasionally forget which room or stall I had even cleaned. I'm pretty sure I cleaned the same section multiple times in one day.

I guess that's what our parents must feel like when cleaning up our messes.

Days began to blend together, as every day seemed to be the same. I would run to work early in the morning, clean all day, run back home, and finally sleep for only a couple hours. My brain was so exhausted I hardly even noticed the bad things going on around me. Over and over again, day after day, nothing seemed to change. I got so used to the cleaning that I could zone completely out and still work just as hard. I once went through an entire day without being able to remember a single thing about it. The only reason I knew I actually worked was because Jimmy was observing me all day, and there's no way he'd let me get away with anything.

When I zoned out, I mainly thought about my past. I really began to miss my family. I missed sitting down on the porch and talking about our day. I missed playing catch with my dad in the park, talking about old cars with my grandpa, and even answering the million questions Grandma had for me. I missed our safe neighborhoods, the way Mr. Jones's windows would shine, and the clean streets. But most of all, I missed smiling faces and that occasional "How are you?" as strangers walked by each other. It was difficult to remember what it felt like to have someone truly care about me. I couldn't remember the last time I saw someone show any sort of love, compassion, or respect for another person. The more I thought about it, the more depressed I got.

I didn't know how things could've gotten any worse, but they sure did. At first, everything followed the normal routine. I ran to work and cleaned all day. Like normal, when my work day was over, I would always confirm when I was needed next. If anything was for sure, I knew I was expected to be there bright and early the next morning, usually around 4:00. It felt like a luxury if I was told 4:30 instead, but that rarely ever happened. Then, to finish my day at the farm, I would get my money. I quickly learned that I couldn't trust anyone anymore, so as soon as I got the money, I counted it. I could tell that made the farmer angry, but I didn't care. I needed every possible dollar I could get. Ever since my first day, he kept to his word, and paid me seven bucks an hour. But on this day, I saw that the cash didn't add up. I didn't even have to count to notice. When I added up my hours, I calculated that I was only paid four bucks an hour.

"I'm sorry, sir, but I noticed I'm missing some money," I said to the farmer.

"How did you lose your money already?" he asked me.

"I didn't lose it. I just opened it to count it, and I only see $64," I said.

"That's what I gave you. You better walk away with what you have, kid," he yelled angrily. I could tell he knew what he was doing. I knew better than to keep talking about it, but I worked way too hard for him to shorthand me, and I needed the money.

Deprived of sleep, exhausted from my day, and tired of the mistreatment, I exploded. "I work hard all day for you!" I yelled. "I worked 16 hours today. That should be $112!"

The next thing I knew, my head was lying flat on the ground, caked in mud. At first, I wasn't sure what happened, I was so dazed and confused. But when I looked back up at my boss and saw him shaking his own hand in pain, I knew he hit me good. I hoped it hurt him as bad as it hurt my face, but I knew that wasn't possible. He hit me so hard, I couldn't see straight, and my face throbbed so badly, it felt like I had been run over by a herd of buffalo. For an old guy, he sure could hit hard.

"Who do you think you are, talking to me like that?" he asked. I obviously knew not to say anything at that moment, so I just stayed on the ground and kept my mouth shut, although I'm not sure I could have talked anyways.

"I'll pay you whatever I want to, and there's nothing you can do about it!" he screamed. "You hear me?!" I could tell he was getting even angrier as he went on. "I don't know what world you're living in, but I can easily replace you. Now, get out of here!"

Still completely stunned by his hit, it took me awhile to get up, yet he didn't move the entire time. He continued to stare me down, dead set on making sure I left without saying another word, which of course I wasn't going to do. It looked like he was about to explode, and I wasn't about to push him any further. When I finally built up the strength to stand up, I quickly wiped the mud off my face, tucked the money in my socks, and started my jog home.

CHAPTER 12

The Other Side

The faster I ran home, the more worked up I got. I decided it was probably better to just slow myself down and cool off, so I could actually process what to do next. I was so mad at the farmer and probably even madder at the fact that I couldn't do anything about it. I also knew I was no longer on his good side, if there even was such a thing, so there really wasn't much hope for me anymore. I knew if I stood up to him, he'd knock me senseless again, then probably shorthand me again, or even fire me. There wasn't anyone to hold him accountable for what he was doing to me or to the other workers, so he could do whatever he wanted. If I decided to try out something else, I was confident that it wouldn't be any different, other than the fact that I'd have to meet new, most likely mean, people.

My thoughts were racing, and just like at work, I began to think about the glorious past. I just didn't want to see any more greedy, selfish people, and I didn't know if I could take looking at one more negative face. Was it too much to ask for just one smile? Just one! I never thought I'd miss a smile so much, but the way people were treating each other around here wore me down. I couldn't take it anymore.

As I continued to walk home, Mrs. Porter came to my mind, which was a complete surprise. With everything that was going on, I really didn't have time to sit down and think about much. It seemed like life was moving so fast, and all I could do was try to keep up to survive. But Mrs. Porter's message was overtaking my thoughts. I could still remember every word from her little slip of paper.

"A selfish world is a world full of careless acts, disrespect, and greedy behavior. A selfless world is a world full of love, respect, and passion for others," I said to myself. It all made sense now. She had me so worked up in her lesson, but I realized I never truly understood her message. "A selfish world is a world full of careless acts, disrespect, and greedy behavior," I said again. I remember thinking that I never wanted to live in a selfish world, but I probably didn't understand the magnitude of such a world. Now I did. Careless acts...disrespect...greedy behavior.... It was everywhere in front of me, and it was an everyday thing that I couldn't escape. No one was safe, and no one was loved. What a horrible world it had become. The discouragement I felt brought me to an all-time low.

"What am I supposed to do?!" I cried out, knowing that no one would pay any attention to what I was saying anyway. They never did.

Before I could take another step forward, I felt a foot pop out and kick my foot out from underneath me. Catching me completely off guard, it sent me nose diving into the cement sidewalk. It was so unexpected, I hardly had any time to catch myself, so I wasn't able to stop my nose from smashing into the hard cement. I instantly felt the warm blood running out of my nose, and as I turned around to look up, I saw three older boys standing over me. I was so deep in thought, I wasn't paying attention to my surroundings, but I still couldn't believe I didn't see them. As I scanned around to figure out what was happening and where the boys had come from, I saw that there was a shop next to me, with its door cracked open. I figured they must have hidden behind that door, but I couldn't understand why they chose to ambush me. Not wanting to look weak, I stood up as quickly as I could.

"You work hard at the farm today?" one of the boys asked. I could tell by his size that he was the leader. I didn't know how old he was, but he was big, and there weren't many people that would mess with him. The other two boys were a couple steps back, just waiting for his direction. But I thought it was an odd question for him to ask me, and I was confused on how he knew I worked at the farm. I'd never seen any of them before.

"I always work hard," I said, hoping to get them away from me. I wasn't sure what else to say.

"Well, I'll make this really easy for you. Just hand me your money," he said.

"I don't have any money on me," I responded. Knowing I had hidden my money in a good spot, I figured I could easily show them I didn't have any.

Without saying another word, and without giving me a chance to protect myself, he wound up and punched me right in the stomach. It was so fast that I didn't have time to move at all. It dropped me so quickly and made it so difficult for me to breathe that I just knelt on the ground gasping for air. While I was down, I hoped that maybe just once, someone watching or walking by would stop to help. But of course, no one did.

"If I were you, I would be a little more careful with what I say," he yelled at me. "I've been watching you go back and forth from the farm, and I've watched you get paid every day after work. You better just hand us your money, or we'll take it from you."

When I got the strength to stand and look him in the eyes, I knew I had two options. I could give him my hard-earned money, or I could run for it. Since I ran every day back and forth from work, I was in pretty good shape. And I was fast. There weren't many people that could outrun me. He and I stared at each other for a good 30 seconds, but what sealed the deal for me was when I watched him turn to look at the other two behind him.

Just like I was stealing a base in a baseball game, I took off like a rocket on a mission. With them to my back, I ran as fast as I possibly could. We were zigzagging through all kinds of crowds, hurdling the trash cans laid out on the streets, and doing whatever was necessary to go faster. I figured I'd be able to lose them within a couple blocks, but every time I looked back, I saw them getting closer and closer. By the time I realized they were in just as good of shape as I was, they were almost right on top of me. I could hear every breath they took, and it sounded like a fine-tuned engine that was not about to slow down.

As we got closer to my house, I was worried about showing them where I lived. If they found out where I lived, they could get me anytime they wanted. To try to throw them for a loop, I began taking side streets and alleyways, anything to slow them down and get them off my back. Finally, after so many blocks of running, I felt the distance between us growing. I knew not to slow down, but I could feel my confidence rising, and I knew with the distance that all I had to do was turn down one more alley.

I rounded one more corner into my final alley, when I saw a large black puddle of oil in front of me. I tried so hard to miss the puddle, but I just didn't see it in time. I had so much speed going into the puddle that I couldn't stop my momentum. My feet slipped out from under me, sending me right into a dumpster. It felt like a thousand needles went through my shoulder, as I smashed it into that dumpster. The pain was unreal, and I couldn't help but scream, but even worse was knowing that they were still coming for me.

With everything I had, I tried to crawl away, but I had nothing left. I felt their hands grab me by the ankles and pick me up.

"You just made a big mistake," the leader yelled at me. I knew my run was over, and at that point, I just hoped they would take my money and leave. "Where's the money?!" he yelled.

Before giving me a chance to tell him, they threw me back on the ground and started searching for it. They went through all my pockets, tugged and ripped my clothes, and if I even moved at all, they

made me pay for it immediately. I was in so
much pain from the dumpster that I wasn't
able to do anything, and after taking hit
after hit, I wasn't able to tell them where it
was either. I tried multiple times, but I
wasn't given the chance again. Finally, they
found my money just inside my sock, and as
quickly as it started, they bolted out of
there, leaving me in the worst shape of my
life.

Bruised...beaten...lifeless. I tried to
scream for help, but I couldn't produce any
words. Beyond exhausted and hurt, even
the slightest movements were impossible. I
just lay there helpless, hoping for someone
to see me.

Hardly able to keep my eyes open, I
began to hear footsteps coming towards
me. They seemed like they were moving so
fast that I was worried they wouldn't stop.
Then I saw—though my eyes were blurry,
I saw him, and I knew instantly who he was.

I saw a boy with blonde hair. I could make out his black and red shorts and his orange t-shirt. Then, the most obvious of all, I saw his green baseball hat.

Though I knew he wouldn't help me, I couldn't help but hope. Though I knew better than anyone what he was thinking, I wanted so badly for him to change his decision. I wanted to say, "Forget about yourself, show some compassion!" But I knew that wasn't going to work.

The pain became unbearable, and my eyes were so heavy I couldn't hold on any longer. As my eyes finally closed, I heard his hand smack hard against the dumpster, and, knowing exactly what was next, I heard his voice yell, "Help, help!"

After all I'd been through, I realized this was the most selfish act of all, and the fact that it came from him, broke my heart. How could he? How could I?

CHAPTER 13

Our World

Like a character rejuvenating in a video game, I felt my strength coming back. The pain was slowly subsiding, and I could open my eyes again. When I opened them, the blur had also faded, and everything seemed so clear. I looked around and noticed I was sitting in a chair in a strange room, a room I did not recognize. There wasn't any other furniture or anything on the walls at all. Then, like a little kid looking at his presents on Christmas morning, I turned around and stared at the most beautiful thing I'd seen in a long time. It was just a door—probably a door that everyone was used to seeing, but this one was red, and one that I remembered very well. I remembered the last time I went through that door, and how my world completely changed when I did.

The excitement I felt from seeing that door overcame me, and without taking even another second to look at it, I opened that door and ran out of the room. Sounding like a crack of thunder, I heard the over-whelming chants begin, and I saw the thousands and thousands of people staring at me from their views in the stadium. Just like I remembered, not a single person smiled. All I saw were angry and depressed frowns, yet it didn't bother me at all. Deep inside, I knew that was about to change.

"A selfish world is a world full of careless acts, disrespect, and greedy behavior," they chanted.

I hauled it down the long aisle, as fast as I possibly could. I knew it would be a long run, but I didn't care at all. I thought about everything that I'd been through and all the things I missed, pushing me to run even faster. Every stride, every step, was just as exciting as the first. Then, there it was, an even more exciting door. A door that brought me to tears, because I knew my world was changing again, and this time, for the better. I never thought I'd be excited about a door. It sounds funny just thinking about it, but this yellow door meant so much more. I knew hidden behind it was a world I took advantage of, where there were people who actually cared about others. A world I could help make better by showing compassion for the people around me.

Like music to my ears, I realized the chanting from the people had changed.

"A selfless world is a world full of love, respect, and passion for others," they said. It felt so good to hear those words, but perhaps even better were the thousands of joyful people smiling at me. These were true meaningful smiles that were meant to uplift others, and they made me feel so much joy. It was a feeling I would never forget and something I hoped I could help others feel as well.

My grandma used to get after me for throwing doors open and flying through them before I checked what was ahead of me, but in this case, I couldn't wait any longer. I twisted the doorknob and bolted through the yellow door lightning fast. The room was so bright, and it blinded me momentarily. It felt like I was staring into the sun, so I had to close my eyes right away.

While my eyes were closed, I saw my eyelids darkening back to normal, as if a cloud had covered the sun, so I knew I was in the clear to open my eyes again.

As I opened my eyes, I was incredulous. Everything was so familiar, from the heap of clean clothes my grandma left for me, to my green hat I put on my bed stand. I even saw Mrs. Porter's note right on the pillow next to me. My nightmare was over. I was home...I was back.

So full of energy, I popped out of my bed and dashed down the stairs. I never thought I'd be so excited to see my grandparents again, but I had missed them more than anything.

"Grandma! Grandpa!" I yelled. "Where are you?" I hadn't seen them in so long, I kind of forgot their daily routine, which they very rarely broke from.

"We are in the kitchen. Why on earth are you yelling?" Grandma asked.

I don't know if her voice always sounded so sweet, but at that moment, it was the sweetest voice you'd ever hear. I didn't care what kind of questions she had ready for me or what crazy story she'd come up with—I just wanted to be with her and Grandpa.

I think I spooked them with how quickly I ran into the kitchen, and I about wiped out because of the slippery floor, but as soon as my feet were stable, I gave Grandma the biggest hug. "I missed you, Grandma," I said, "Thank you so much for everything you do for me!"

I could tell Grandma was confused, but her eyes were gleaming with joy. "How could you miss me?" she asked while laughing, "I never went anywhere."

Knowing it would take too long to explain everything to her, and knowing she wouldn't understand anyway, I turned to Grandpa and gave him a bear hug as well. "I missed you, too Grandpa. I'm so happy to see you both," I said. I could tell Grandpa was just as confused as Grandma, but the way his face brightened up was priceless.

"Do you guys care if I go outside for a bit?" I asked. I was anxious to see what everything looked like outside. I wanted to see our beautiful street again, with Mr. Jones's clean windows, and I wanted to see people's smiling faces.

"Of course, Brandon," Grandma said.

When I walked outside, I was in awe. I had forgotten how beautiful the buildings around us were, and I was so happy to see how clean everything was. When I checked on Mr. Jones's windows, they were even cleaner than I remembered. Better yet, Mr. Jones was in his shop greeting people like he normally did, with a huge, encouraging smile. He was right—his smile really did make you feel good about yourself.

The streets and sidewalks were full of people, people who felt safe walking around the city. There were people opening doors for complete strangers, people who helped carry bags for each other, and people who helped others who were hurting. There were people who cared for others, who treated others with respect, and showed compassion. People who were selfless.

As I watched the people going by, I thought again about Mrs. Porter. I remembered her telling us, "This is your world now. You can either choose to be that selfish person who walks past others, or you can choose to be selfless and show that you care for others."

She was right. This was our world now, and what I do now and in the future impacts our world. I decided that I needed to be that smile for people to see, the one who makes them feel respected, valued, and encouraged. I needed to be a person who would stop what I was doing to help someone in need. I needed to be someone who puts others first, even when it seems inconvenient, because that's the type of world I want to live in.

Lifeless

"A selfless world is a world full of love, respect, and passion for others," I said to myself, and what a great world that truly is.

Brandon Bowman

ABOUT THE AUTHOR

Brandon Bowman, a graduate of Ferris State University, is an
elementary teacher and author, with a strong passion for teaching
students the love and joy of reading and writing. Brandon was born
and raised in the northern part of the beautiful state of Michigan, and
he has always loved anything to do with sports, nature and wildlife,
and adventure. He is the middle child in a large family of nine
children. His family has always been the centerpiece of his hobbies
and passions, leading him to the love and passion for elementary
education. Now a father of three beautiful children, and a teacher who
cherishes the relationships he forms with his students, his goal is that
students would not just engage in reading and writing, but find the
joy, excitement, and adventure that comes with it.

Made in the USA
Middletown, DE
22 November 2022